AGENT ARTHUR'S JUNGLE JOURNEY

Martin Oliver

Illustrated by

Paddy Mounter

Designed by

Paddy Mounter, Kim Blundell and Brian Robertson

Series Editor: Gaby Waters

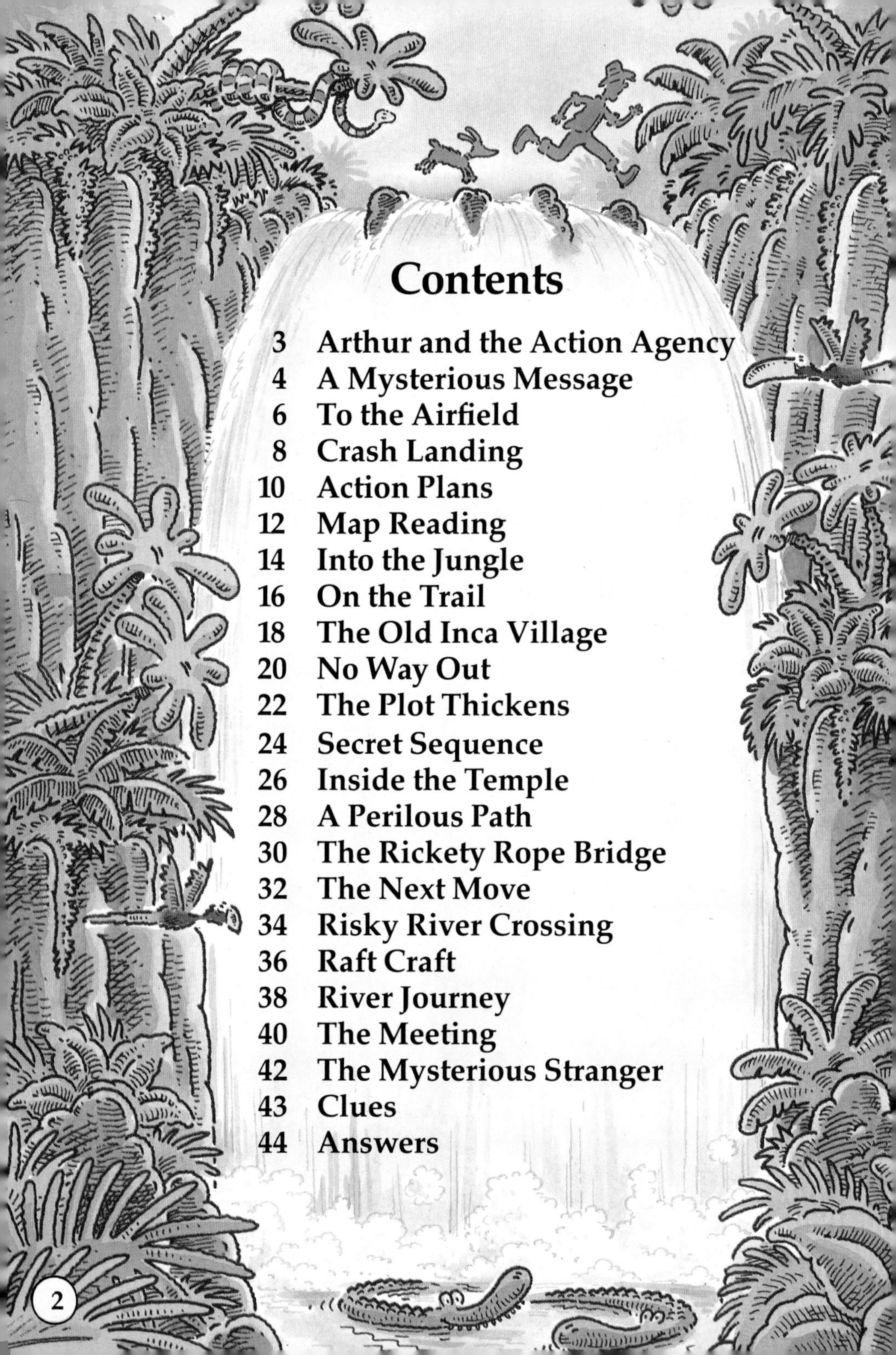

Contents

Arthur and the Action Agency

The Action Agency is a world wide undercover organization dedicated to fighting crime and solving mysteries. Supremely successful, the Agency lives up to its motto, *Search, Solve and Survive*, by operating a "go anywhere, do anything" service.

Arthur is the newest and youngest recruit to the Action Agency and this story follows his first mission. Arthur's uncle is Jake Sharpe, the founder and brains of the Agency. He is an elusive figure and a master of disguise, rarely seen but always respected.

You can take part in Arthur's adventure by solving the fun but tricky puzzles that appear on almost every page. Clues to the answers and vital information lurk in the pictures and the words. If you get stuck, you will find extra clues and all the answers at the back of the book.

A Mysterious Message

Agent Arthur was sitting in a small office of the Action Agency. But there wasn't much action going on. In fact, except for Arthur and his dog Sleuth, no one had walked through the door for weeks and weeks.

It was summer and Arthur had been left minding the office while his Uncle Jake was away on a top secret mission. His uncle was often away for weeks, months and sometimes years on end. Meanwhile, Arthur stayed put.

Arthur was reading a comic book, dreaming about having adventures like Uncle Jake, when CRASH . . . something hurtled through the window and whistled past his left ear. He dived for cover.

Ten seconds later, Arthur peered out from behind the desk. Papers were scattered everywhere. Among them was a half-brick. Sleuth sniffed the brick warily, while Arthur cautiously removed a piece of paper wrapped round it. He saw strange signs scrawled on it – the unmistakeable symbols of the Agency Action Code.

What does the message say?

MISSION INSTRUCTIONS FOR
MON 16
MISSING
Jane Printz, the schoolgirl photographer, has disappeared in the South American jungle while photographing the rare Orchid Narcotica.
Jane Printz
CROOKFAX
Name:
HENRIK HITMAN
Hired assassin
This Man is
and will sh
Last seen in
CROOKFAX
Name:
RICK J.
ELDT.
CROOKFAX
Name:
EL PAUNCHO
also called 'The Boss'
Master criminal. Suspected links with notorious 'SPIDER' organization.

To the Airfield

Arthur looked outside. The stone-thrower was nowhere to be seen.

This was it. Action! Arthur studied his map and eagerly pulled on a jacket.

He crammed a helmet on his head and raced Sleuth downstairs.

He spun round and spotted the base. They sneaked closer and keeping under cover, circled round the perimeter fence.

"What's going on?" thought Arthur, scanning the base suspiciously. "We must get on to the plane to find out."

They leapt onto the bike. Arthur pedalled and the motor choked into life.

Sleuth hung on as they zoomed down busy streets and roared out of town.

At last, Arthur stopped to recheck the map. He felt a tap on his back.

But how? Then Arthur spotted a gap in the fence. They could crawl through it safely, but they still had to get past the mean-looking guards without being spotted.

Find a safe route onto the plane.

Crash Landing

Arthur and Sleuth sneaked aboard the plane. Suddenly the door slammed shut behind them.

The plane's engines roared. Arthur and Sleuth stared out of the window in horror. They were moving.

Arthur hung on to a heavy wooden crate as the plane rattled and jolted along the bumpy runway.

Sleuth watched as Arthur shouted and banged on the cockpit door. It was no good. After a few minutes Arthur slumped down beside Sleuth.

"We'd better get comfortable," he said. "It might be a long flight."

Sleuth snorted in disgust as the plane flew on into the night.

Suddenly Arthur woke up. Sleuth was still dozing, but something was wrong.

The plane shook violently and began to nose-dive with one engine ablaze.

There was just time to wake Sleuth and get into emergency landing positions . . .

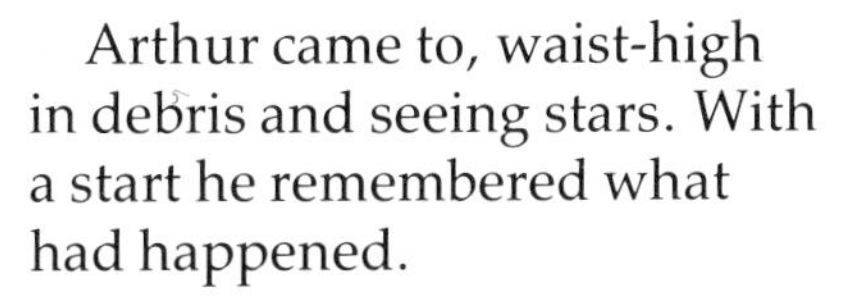

Arthur came to, waist-high in debris and seeing stars. With a start he remembered what had happened.

Where was Sleuth? Arthur spotted a familiar ear and dug him out of the wreckage. He was dazed, but OK.

They searched for the pilot. Arthur and Sleuth scrambled through the fuselage into the cockpit. It was empty, except for a large stripy snake that hissed and slithered.

Where were they? Arthur peered out of a hole in the smashed windshield. On all sides he could see a thick green jungle of trees, vines and spiky bushes. He gulped. They were alone, somewhere in a dense, tropical rainforest.

Action Plans

Arthur thought back to his Basic Training and knew immediately what to do. He must send a rescue message. But the radio was beyond repair.

Arthur leapt down from the plane. Sleuth stuck his nose out of the cabin to examine the crash site and barked angrily at a vulture circling overhead.

"Never fear," said Arthur, as he began cutting and gathering wood for fires. "We'll move into Plan Two – ground-to-air signals."

Arthur charged through the wreckage, making flags, laying out messages and shifting huge pieces of reflective metal.

"Finished at last," said Arthur, thinking how proud his Action Training Instructor would be. "Now we wait to be rescued."

Meanwhile, Sleuth was nosing about in the cockpit. He barked loudly and bounced out of the plane carrying a big black briefcase.

"Can't you see I'm busy being lookout?" Arthur asked, grumpily dumping out the case.

"This is useless," he said, waving a piece of paper covered in unusual writing. "Unless ... unless ... it's in code!"

Can you decode the message?

Map Reading

Arthur realized that they were on their own, with no hope of rescue . . . This was his big chance! Now he could use his Action Agency Training to pit his wits against whatever dangers he might encounter in the hostile jungle.

"Being intrepid Action Agents, we will investigate any suspicious goings-on at the base," Arthur said bravely. "But first we must find our position on this map."

Arthur knew that he could pinpoint their position, if only he could see some landmarks.

But how? They were hemmed in by thick jungle on all sides. Arthur sprang into action. He took a deep breath and scrambled up a steep, rocky hill, with trees growing on the summit.

At last he reached the top and peered through the trees. Sleuth was just a worried-looking dot down below, but Arthur could see for miles around. He pulled a map and compass out of his pockets.

Where are Arthur and Sleuth? Can you find the base?

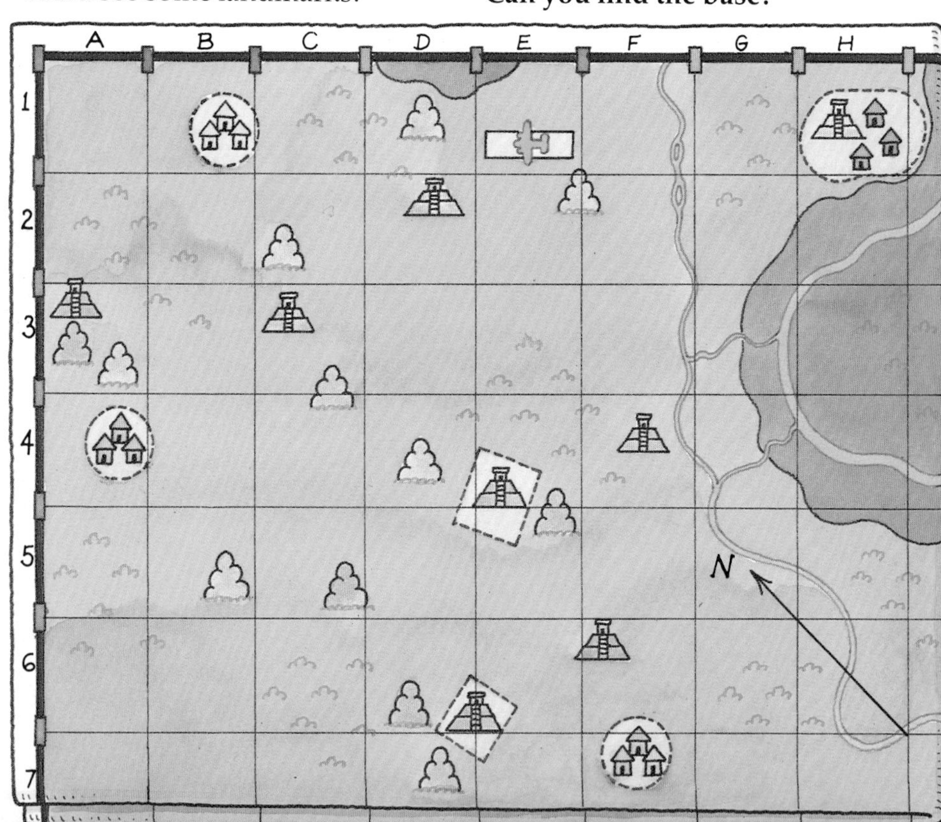

Into the Jungle

Arthur clambered back down to Sleuth and they hunted through the plane for useful equipment to make up a survival kit. Soon they were ready for the trek into the dense jungle.

Arthur strode forward, firmly gripping the handle of his machete. He hacked through the thick leaves and vines that barred their path. Huge trees towered over them and ear-splitting monkey calls shattered the silence.

They stumbled over fallen trees and waded through rotting leaves. Arthur looked back as the plane disappeared behind some spiky bushes. The jungle swallowed them up. He whistled to cheer himself up. Sleuth joined in with a loud growl.

From all around came rustling and slithering noises. Green eyes glinted menacingly at them. But there was no time to wonder about what was lurking in the undergrowth, as large raindrops began to splash down through the trees. Within minutes Arthur and Sleuth were soaked, but still they trudged on through hordes of hungry mosquitoes.

"Over there," gasped Arthur, as the rain stopped at last. "We'll rest for a bit."

They slipped and slid towards a tree trunk. Suddenly Arthur caught sight of something very unusual. He sprinted towards it, just as Sleuth barked a warning.

What has Arthur spotted?
What has Sleuth spotted?

Grrr

On the Trail

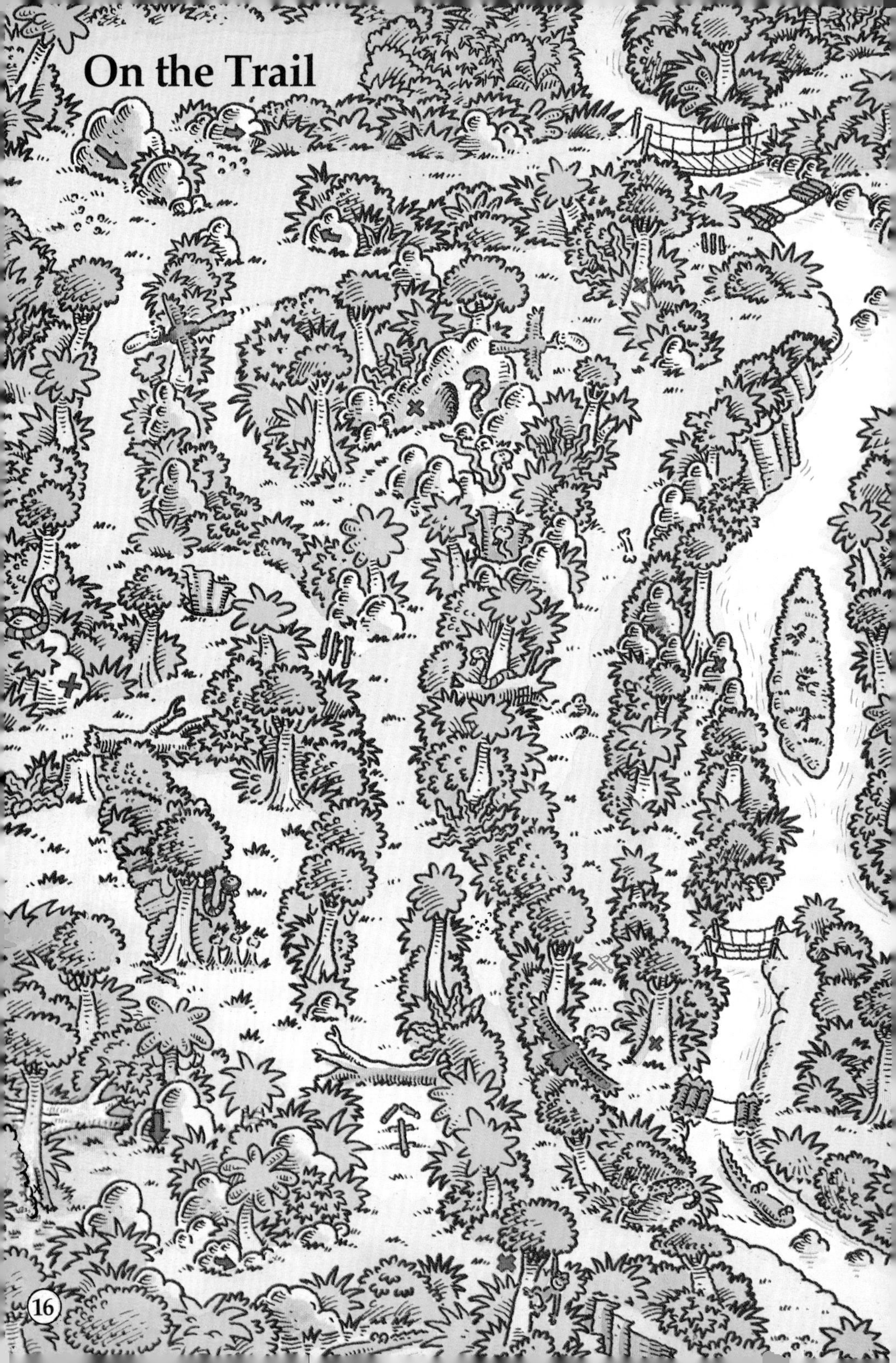

Arthur skidded to a halt, just in time to avoid the snake and a concealed patch of swampy ground. He crept over to examine the sign. It was a cross, painted on the tree trunk.

"It's a warning danger sign," he said, staring at the marsh.

If there was one sign, perhaps there were more. Arthur and Sleuth looked around. Opposite them was a fallen tree and a large rock. There was an arrow on the rock which pointed down towards a rough track that bent round in a U-shape.

"It's a trail," exclaimed Arthur. "It must lead to the base. Let's follow it."

Where are Arthur and Sleuth? Can you follow the trail?

The Old Inca Village

The trail led up a steep hill and ended abruptly at a stone wall. Below them was an old Inca village. This was the base they were searching for!

The smell of cooking came towards them. Sleuth's stomach began to rumble. He was just about to leap over the wall when he felt a hand on his collar.

"Get down Sleuth," Arthur hissed, as he stared at the armed men in the village. "Whatever they're doing here, I don't like the look of it."

Arthur's eyes narrowed. One of the men looked familiar. Arthur was sure he had seen him before.

Which man does Arthur recognize?

No Way Out

Arthur and Sleuth ducked out of sight and crept back into the jungle.

"Let's wait until dark and then move in," whispered Arthur. "But we must be careful."

He stepped forward. Suddenly a rope fastened round his ankle and he was hoisted up into the air. Everything went black.

When Arthur opened his eyes, he was lying on the ground, his head throbbing. He tried to stand up, but couldn't. His hands and feet were securely bound with strong rope.

A dark shadow loomed over him and Arthur stared up at the short, ugly figure of El Pauncho. Arthur didn't like his face, or the sound of what he was saying.

But there was no time to worry. Arthur was picked up by two guards who carried him through the village and threw him into a dingy hut.

Arthur's brain whirred. What was Pauncho doing in the jungle? Where was Sleuth? But before he could think straight, the hut began spinning and Arthur's head hit the floor.

It was dark when Arthur woke up. He blinked quickly to get used to the moonlight and staggered to his feet. No prison hut could hold an Action Agent. He must escape, but how? The walls were thick and there was a chunky lock on the door.

Arthur struggled to undo the knots around his hands and feet. It was no good. The ropes were too tight. He clenched his fists. He was trapped. There seemed to be no way out.

How can Arthur escape?

The Plot Thickens

Arthur slid down the rough thatch and landed on the ground with a thud. The camp was quiet. He was free to look for Sleuth and to discover what dirty work Paucho was up to.

Keeping to the shadows, Arthur crept through the camp. He dodged from cover to cover. There was a noise behind him . . . but it was only someone snoring.

With all senses at red alert, he crept past a lighted window, right under the noses of Paucho and his side-kick.

Arthur's ears pricked up at what he heard. Paucho was plotting something sinister. If only Arthur could work out what.

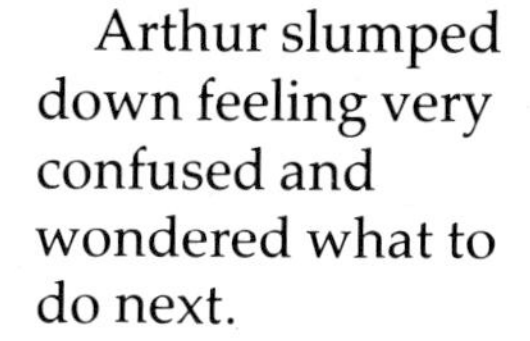

Arthur slumped down feeling very confused and wondered what to do next.

Suddenly, he heard footsteps. He turned, alarmed, to find himself nose to nose with Sleuth.

Sleuth jumped up wagging his tail furiously and dropped the sharp knife he had been carrying.

Arthur picked up the knife. There was a piece of paper tied round the handle. On it was a plan of the base and a message. Arthur groaned as he read it. All his great escape work had been unnecessary. But who was this friend in Pauncho's camp?

Arthur studied the map and tried to work out where he was. He thought back to his first view of the base and knew which hut he should go to.

Where is Arthur? Which hut is the one marked X on the map?

Secret Sequence

Sleuth led Arthur to where he had hidden their survival kit and, fully prepared, they tiptoed to the meeting place. Suddenly Arthur froze. He spotted a sinister shadow. It was creeping towards them. They were trapped. CLICK . . .

"Nice photo," whispered a cheerful voice. "I'm a friend. My name's Jane Printz."

"The missing photographer," gasped Arthur, handing back the knife. "What are you doing here?"

"I was in the jungle taking photos of the rare Orchid Narcotica," replied Jane, putting the knife in her bag, and handing Arthur a series of photos. "When I came across this base, I realized that something very suspicious was going on."

What was going on? Arthur studied Jane's photos, trying to piece the story together. Suddenly Sleuth growled a warning. They dived for cover as Paumcho and his henchmen marched past towards an old temple covered in vines.

Paumcho pressed four numbered buttons on a panel. Top left, bottom left, Arthur blinked and missed the third, then top right. A heavy steel door opened, the men stepped inside and the door clanged shut.

"Let's follow them," Arthur said. "But what is the sequence that will open the door?"

Can you work out what is going on from the photos?
What is the secret sequence?

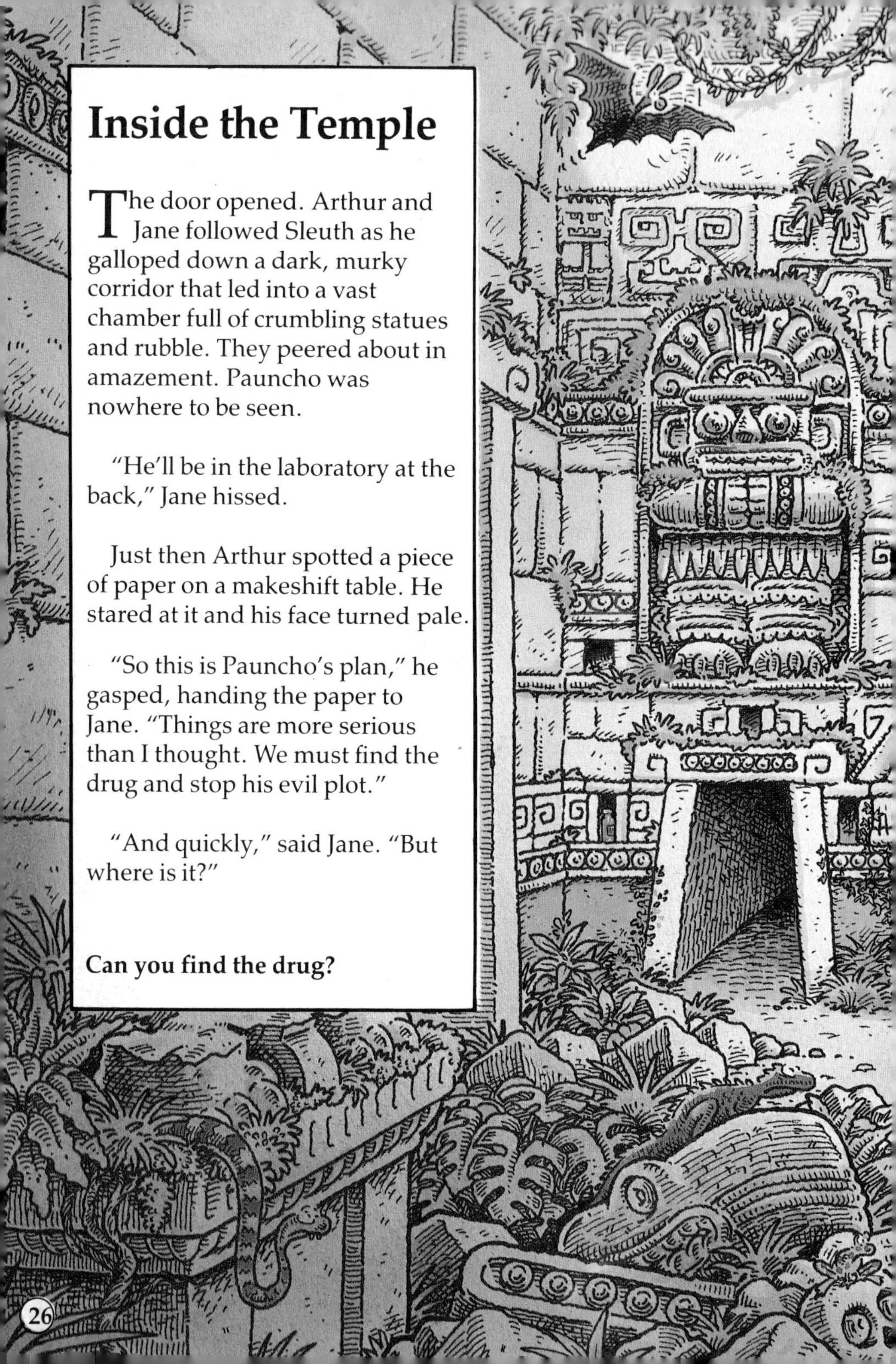

Inside the Temple

The door opened. Arthur and Jane followed Sleuth as he galloped down a dark, murky corridor that led into a vast chamber full of crumbling statues and rubble. They peered about in amazement. Pauncho was nowhere to be seen.

"He'll be in the laboratory at the back," Jane hissed.

Just then Arthur spotted a piece of paper on a makeshift table. He stared at it and his face turned pale.

"So this is Pauncho's plan," he gasped, handing the paper to Jane. "Things are more serious than I thought. We must find the drug and stop his evil plot."

"And quickly," said Jane. "But where is it?"

Can you find the drug?

EL PAUNCHO TO SPIDER ORGANIZATION
PREPARATORY PHASE OF WORLD DOMINATION PROGRAMME NOW COMPLETE. FIRST BOTTLE OF MCD (MIND CONTROL DRUG) NOW READY FOR TESTS. INITIAL DRIP SAMPLES SUGGEST A POWER MANY TIMES GREATER THAN ESTIMATED (BRAIN-WASH FORCE FACTOR 15) AND WITH PERMANENT EFFECTS.
HANDOVER ARRANGEMENTS: OLD SHACK AT CO-ORDINATES 5·3, 1·3. WEDNESDAY 16·00. CASH AS ARRANGED + 10%

A Perilous Path

Jane grabbed the drug and gently placed it in her pocket.

"Come on," whispered Arthur. "Let's get out of here, before Pauncho finds us."

Too late! The room echoed with voices, Pauncho was back. Arthur scuttled down a corridor, waving to the others to follow.

Jane tried to stop him, but Arthur had disappeared into the inky blackness. Jane and Sleuth dashed after him at top speed, brushing away sticky cobwebs and dodging sleeping bats.

Suddenly the passage sloped steeply downhill. The trio raced on until they saw light. Arthur sprinted towards it . . .

. . . out onto a sheer rock face. Down below was a fast-flowing river and treacherous ravines. Arthur trod thin air, but Jane caught hold of his arm and pulled him back to safety.

Behind them came Pauncho's angry shouts and the pounding of feet. They were trapped. There was no way back, only down.

Jane desperately looked around. Opposite them was a cliff with a path leading up it. If they reached the top of the cliff, they might be safe. But how could they get there? Jane looked at the maze of paths.

Can you find a safe route to the top of the cliff opposite?

The Rickety Rope Bridge

They scrambled up the steep path to the top of the cliff. Jane fumbled for her binoculars. There was no time to rest. Pauncho and his men were hot on their trail.

Sleuth raced down the narrow path on the other side of the cliff. Arthur and Jane stumbled after him. Suddenly he started barking. Ahead was a rickety rope bridge over a gorge. Crocodiles were swimming underneath, jaws snapping. Arthur gulped.

"This is the only way across," said Jane, as she and Sleuth stepped gingerly onto the bridge. Arthur followed.

The frail rope bridge began to swing wildly. Jane clung on to the supports and crawled along. Arthur trod carefully, trying not to look down.

"It's not so difficult after all," thought Arthur, halfway across the bridge.

Just then, his foot went through a rotten plank. He tripped and the backpack and machete spiralled down to the crocodiles waiting below. Arthur grabbed a plank and hung on. He hauled himself up inch by painful inch and staggered over to solid ground.

"Safe at last," he gasped.

Bullets whined and ricocheted round him. Jane looked through the binoculars. Pauncho's men were about to cross the bridge.

Arthur knew he had to stop them and started tugging at the pegs. But it was no good – they were dug in too deeply. If only they could cut the ropes.

How can they stop Pauncho's men?

The Next Move

Arthur took charge as he led the trek down into the valley. Progress became slower and slower as the air got hotter and stickier. The steaming vegetation closed in. Every step seemed like a mile through the green foliage.

All of a sudden, there was a deafening thunderclap and raindrops the size of golf balls began to pelt down. Arthur chopped off some leaves to use as umbrellas, while Jane and Sleuth dashed through the jungle, looking for a place to shelter.

They discovered a large hollow tree and scrambled inside. Now to plan the next move.

"Lucky I remembered Rule One of Jungle Journeying," said Arthur, delving into his pockets. "Carry a map and compass at all times."

He triumphantly brandished a map, but the paper was damp and rotten and it fell to pieces.

"We've gone two miles South East from the middle of the rope bridge," he said, trying to fit the pieces of the map together.

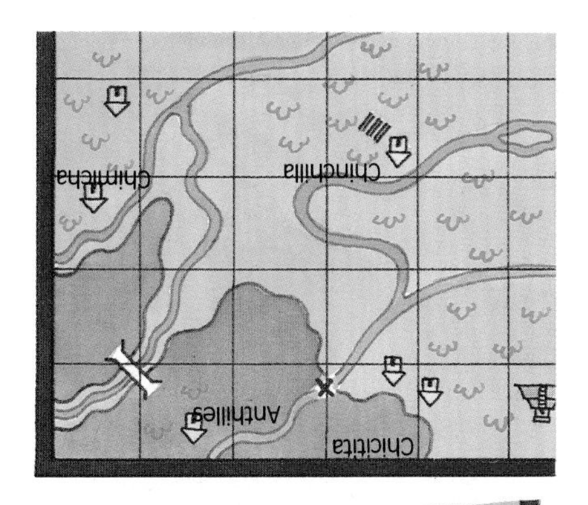

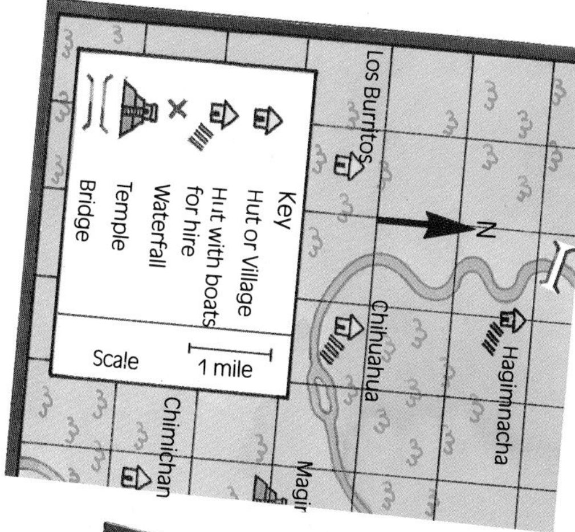

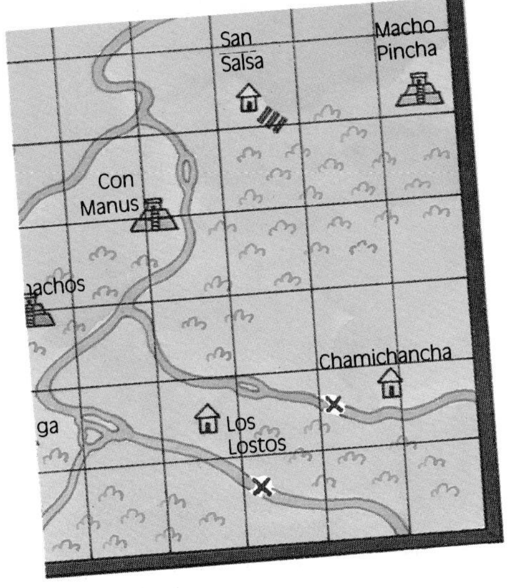

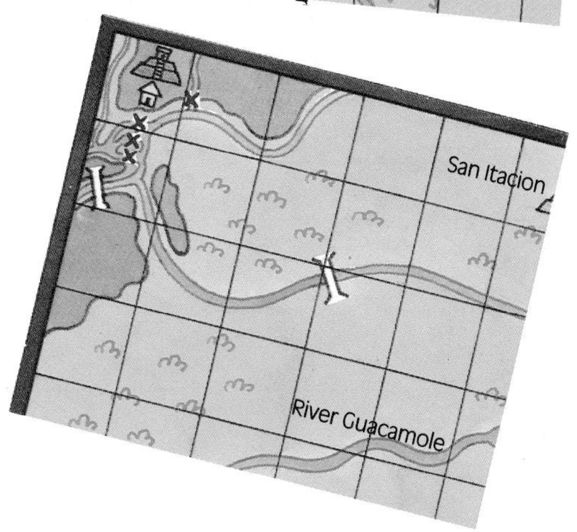

"But where are we heading?" asked Jane.

Arthur looked blank for a second. Then he studied the map and one place name caught his eye. In a flash, he remembered the contact points mentioned in his mission instructions and Agency Memo 521. Today was Wednesday. It was now midday. They had to move fast.

"The quickest way to travel is by river," said Arthur. "But we need a boat."

Together they studied the map and worked out the best route to the nearest Agency contact point.

Where are they?
What is the quickest route to the contact point?

Risky River Crossing

They set off towards the contact point. Arthur checked his compass, Jane read the map and Sleuth barked at swarms of biting insects. They dragged themselves through a muddy mess of rotting leaves as water splashed down from the trees.

On they squelched through sticky black mud until they stopped at the river bank. Where was the bridge? Arthur stared around in horror. It had been washed away by the flooded river. Only a few shattered remains were left.

"It's stopped raining at least," said Jane, peering out from under her leaf. "Let's wait for the water to subside, then we can cross."

"It will take too long," said Arthur, looking at the swollen torrent rushing past.

"We must cross the river to get to the fishing hut," he continued. "If we put our heads together, we're bound to come up with a plan."

Can you find a safe route across the river using Jane's and Arthur's ideas?

Raft Craft

Jane checked that the drug was still safe in her pocket as Sleuth led her and Arthur to a deserted shack made from planks and barrels.

They hunted around for a boat to sail downstream but all they could find was a sunken wreck. Arthur wracked his brains. The only thing to do was to make a raft. But how? He had missed Survival Lesson R for Raft Building and Repairs.

Time was running out for them. Suddenly Sleuth started tugging at Arthur's pocket. There was a ripping noise followed by a dull thud as a heavy book fell to the ground.

"Well done Sleuth," shouted Arthur, grabbing the book and flicking through the pages. "I'd forgotten about this. It's my copy of the Action Agency Survive and Succeed Handbook. It's got raft designs in it."

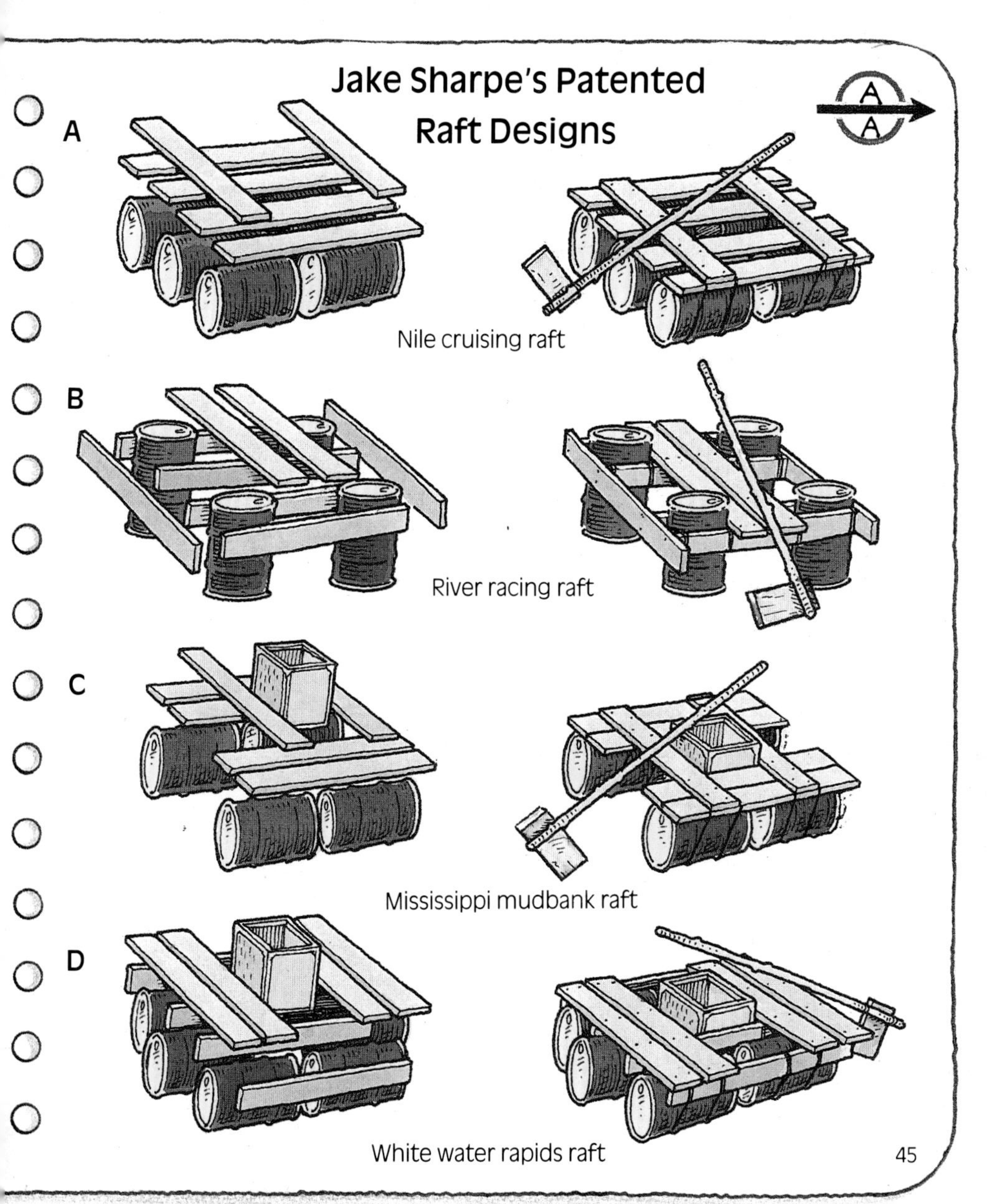

Jane scouted around for raft building materials, while Sleuth sniffed out a hammer, a long coil of rope and some rusty nails. Arthur puzzled over the designs then he checked the equipment that Jane and Sleuth had found.

"It's no good after all," he sighed. "All but four barrels leak and three of the planks are rotten. We can't build a raft."

Is Arthur right?
Can they build a raft?

River Journey

Arthur lashed the final plank into position. Jane prodded the raft gingerly, as Sleuth suspiciously stepped aboard.

"Let's go," shouted Arthur, carrying two bamboo poles. "We're running out of time."

He pushed them clear of the bank, but not clear of trouble. A strong current swept the raft downstream, round mudbanks and through the treacherous waters. Arthur battled to keep them afloat, while Jane and Sleuth fought off the dangers that lay round every corner.

The current began to slacken off. The raft floated on between a triangular island and a small thin island. Suddenly a loud roaring noise filled the air. Waterfalls dead ahead!

"We've got two choices," Arthur said, remembering his Action Agency River Training Course. "We can send the raft downstream and trek overland to meet it. Or we could dismantle the raft and carry it past the falls."

"Neither," said Jane, studying the map. "I know what to do."

What should they do and why?

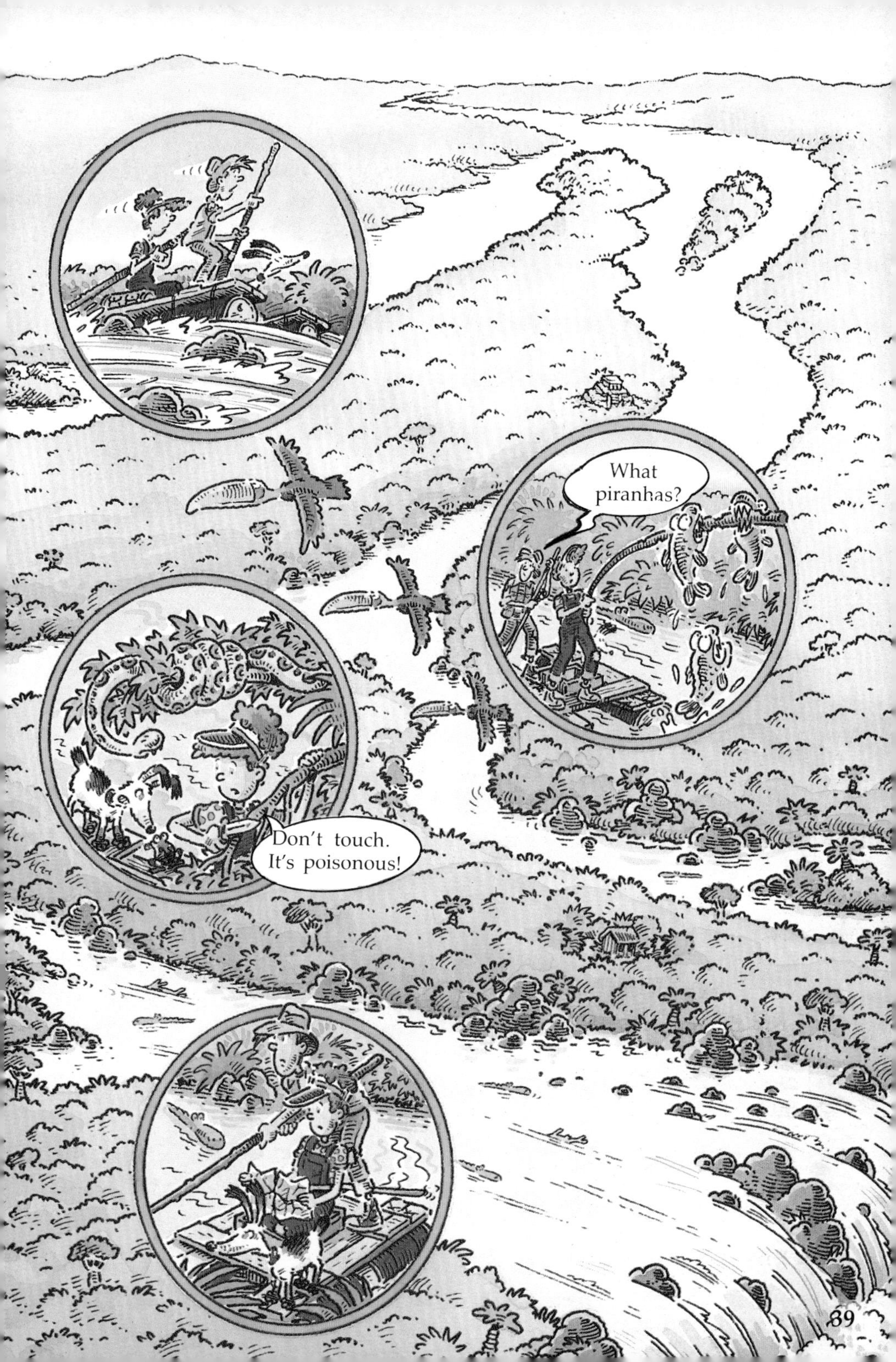
What piranhas?
Don't touch. It's poisonous!

The Meeting

The raft jolted and bumped hard against the river bank throwing Arthur, Jane and Sleuth ashore. They landed in a confused heap.

As they untangled the mess of arms and legs, Jane caught sight of a thatched shack in the middle of a clearing . . . This was the contact point.

"Be careful," whispered Arthur. "We don't know who might be in there."

They tiptoed silently into the clearing, on the look-out for signs of life. Sleuth's nose began to twitch. He growled quietly and scampered towards the hut. Jane and Arthur followed hard on his heels. They peered through a window and gasped in horror.

Inside the hut was . . . Pauncho! Sitting opposite him, at the other end of a long table was a mysterious, crooked looking stranger surrounded by piles of used money.

"We've been set-up," gasped Jane. "The journey was a wild goose chase. We've walked straight into Pauncho's trap."

But Arthur wasn't so sure. His memory flashed back to the conversation he overheard in Pauncho's camp and he scanned the room. Arthur spotted two things that were rather odd.

"Maybe not," he said.

What has Arthur spotted?

The Mysterious Stranger

Arthur sprang into action. With lightning speed, he vaulted through the window, disarmed Pauncho and tied him up.

Then Arthur spun round to confront the stranger and came face to face with . . .

"Uncle Jake!" gasped Arthur. "What are you doing here?"

"Congratulations Arthur and friends," boomed a deep voice. "You've just tied up the loose ends of Operation Orchid."

"A section of the Action Agency Jungle Squad have already cleaned up Pauncho's camp," explained Uncle Jake, "And Pauncho's given us the drug."

"It's a fake," said Arthur, "Jane's got the real stuff."

But Jane's pockets were empty. Where was the drug? Suddenly Sleuth barked.

"Don't worry," smiled Arthur. "We'll find it. Follow that dog."

Where is the drug?

Clues

You will need to hold this page in front of a mirror to read the clues.

Pages 4-5

Look at the Action Code on the pinboard on page 3. A = ω B = Δ

Pages 6-7

First find the gap in the fence. The rest is easy. They can use boxes, crates and sacks as cover, and the music should drown most of the noise they make creeping through the base.

Pages 10-11

Try swapping the first and last letters of each word.

Pages 12-13

The pictures show the view looking due North, South, East and West. Which is which? Try matching the landmarks in the pictures with the landmarks on the map.

Pages 14-15

This is easy. Use your eyes.

Pages 16-17

You don't need a clue for this. Look out for trail signs.

Pages 18-19

Look at the Crookfax papers on page 5.

Pages 20-21

Look at all the things in the hut. What can he use to help him escape?

Pages 22-23

Turn the map the other way up and look at the picture of the base on pages 18-19.

Pages 24-25

The numbers form a sequence, or pattern. The gap between the numbers increases by 1 each time.

Pages 26-27

What does the drug look like? Check the conversation on page 22 and the photo on page 25.

Pages 28-29

This is easy. They can crawl across tree trunks.

Pages 30-31

What was Jane's message attached to? Look back to page 23.

Pages 32-33

This is tricky. Trace or photocopy the map pieces and fit them together. The pictures on pages 28-31 should help you locate the rope bridge on the map. The scale of the map is shown in the key. Look at Arthur's mission instructions on page 5 and Memo 521 on page 3. An anagram is a word made by arranging the letters in a different order.

Pages 34-35

Study each idea in turn. Which ones will work and which will not?

Pages 36-37

How many barrels and planks can they use?

Pages 38-39

Compare the picture with the map on page 33.

Pages 40-41

What was Paunch saying on page 22? Use your eyes.

Page 42

Did Jane drop the bottle somewhere on the journey?

Answers

Pages 4-5

The message is written in Action Code. This is what it says:

MISSION INSTRUCTIONS FOR ACTION AGENT 770. INVESTIGATE CONTENTS OF PLANE AT OLD AIRFIELD. REPORT TO CONTACT POINTS AT QH, DONNOL, WONKYER OR HAGIMNACHIC BY WEDNESDAY 1600 HOURS.

Pages 6-7

The safe route is marked in black.

They crawl behind the sacks and the hut.

Pages 10-11

The message is decoded by swapping the first and last letters of each word. This is what it says:

MIND CONTROL PLAN A. VITAL EQUIPMENT AND SUPPLIES READY FOR TRANSPORTATION ON MONDAY FROM THE OLD AIRFIELD. AIM FOR LANDING STRIP AT E1, THEN PROCEED TO BASE AT H1 VIA MARKED TRAIL. FILE FALSE FLIGHT PLAN. IN CASE OF EMERGENCY, BAIL OUT AND CONTACT BASE. NO RESCUE ATTEMPTS WILL BE MADE. THESE ORDERS ARE ISSUED BY THE BOSS AND MUST BE OBEYED AT ALL COSTS.

Pages 12-13

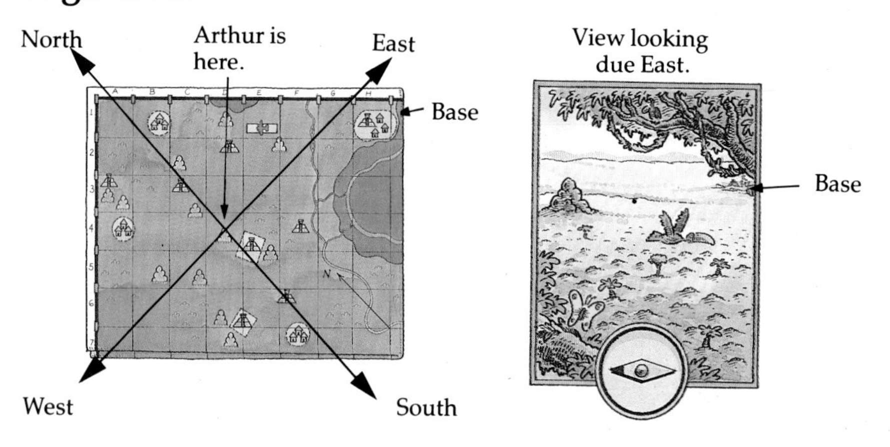

Pages 14-15

Arthur has spotted a cross painted on a tree trunk. Sleuth has spotted a snake.

Pages 16-17

The trail is marked in black.

Sleuth and Arthur are here.

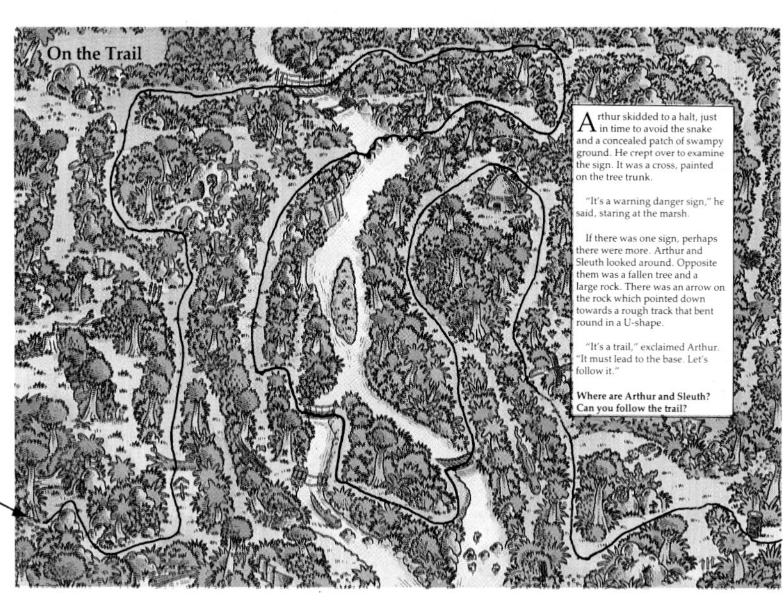

Pages 18-19

Arthur recognizes this man, El Pauncho, from the Action Agency Crookfax on page 5.

Pages 20-21

There are several possible ways to escape, but this is the easiest.

1. Arthur cuts the ropes round his hands with the broken bottle and unties the ropes around his feet.

2. Then he moves a crate to the centre of the hut and climbs onto it.

3. Next he pulls himself up onto the beams and climbs up and out through the hole in the roof.

4. He slides down the thatched roof and jumps to the ground.

Pages 22-23

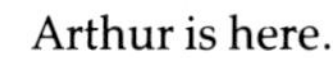

Arthur is here.

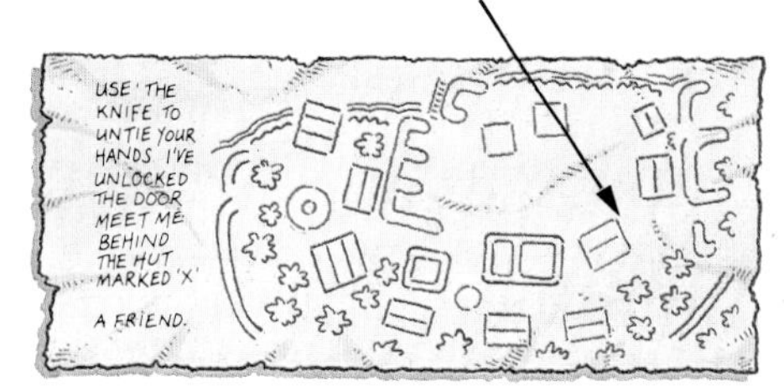

This is the hut marked X on the map.

Pages 24-25

The photos tell a story:

A plane lands in the jungle. El Pauncho and his men step out. Pauncho issues orders which clearly relate to the formula for a powerful mind control drug, made from the extract of the Orchid Narcotica plant. The plants are harvested in the jungle, loaded into baskets and taken to an old temple. Here, one of Pauncho's cronies carries out the distillation process to produce the drug. Then Sleuth and Arthur appear on the scene. Arthur is taken prisoner and Sleuth sets off to rescue him with a message from Jane, wrapped around a knife.

To open the temple door, they need to press the buttons 2, 3, 5 and 8. These numbers form a sequence, or pattern, with the gap between the numbers increasing by 1 each time.

Pages 26-27

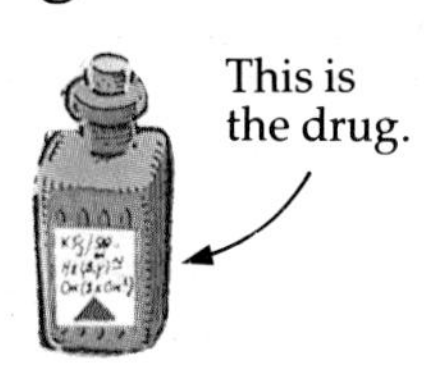

This is the drug.

It is hidden here.

Pages 28-29

The safe route is marked in black.

Pages 30-31

They can cut the ropes securing the bridge with Jane's knife – the one she gave to Sleuth with the message for Arthur (page 23). When Arthur gave the knife back to Jane (page 24), she put it into her bag.

Pages 32-33

The quickest route is marked in black.

They are here.

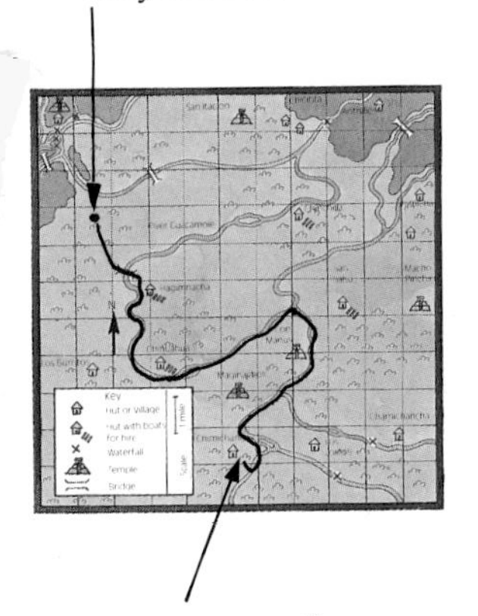

CHIMICHANGA, the contact point.

This is how Arthur worked it all out:

1. He located the rope bridge on the map by thinking back to the landscape nearby (pages 28-31).

2. Then he drew a line twice the length of the one shown in the key running South East from the centre of the bridge.

3. Next he remembered his mission instructions (page 5) which mentioned four possible contact points (QH, DONNOL, WONKYER AND HAGIMNACHIC).

4. Then he remembered the Action Agency Memo 521 (page 3). This is written in Action Code and it says: FROM NOW ON UNTIL FURTHER NOTICE ALL AGENCY CONTACT POINTS WILL BE WRITTEN AS ANAGRAMS.

5. Arthur knew that an anagram is a word made by arranging the letters in a different order and worked out that HAGIMNACHIC is an anagram of CHIMICHANGA.

6. The rest was easy. The quickest route to Chimichanga is by river via the hut with boats for hire marked HAGIMNACHA.

Pages 34-35

Stepping on a crocodile isn't wise.

This is possible but risky. It's easy to lose balance.

The plank is cracked and rotten.

The gap is too wide to jump across.

Pages 36-37

They can build the Mississippi mudbank raft.

Pages 38-39

They have passed the tributary leading to the contact point. They must head for the bank and get off the raft. They can walk along the bank pulling the raft and cross the tributary on the raft. The contact point is a short walk into the jungle.

Pages 40-41

The crooked looking stranger sitting opposite Pauncho has FOUR fingers on each hand, yet Pauncho was planning to meet the man with THREE fingers (page 22). The Action Agency logo is clearly visible on a piece of paper in the man's briefcase.

Page 42

The bottle dropped out of Jane's pocket as they came ashore.

First published in 1988 by
Usborne Publishing Ltd,
83-85 Saffron Hill,
London EC1N 8RT, England.

Printed in Italy. American edition 1988.